Serving the
Children
of the World

The Coiled Viper

A Magical World Awaits You
Read

THE SECRETS OF DROON

THE SECRETS OF DROON

The Coiled Viper

by Tony Abbott

Illustrated by Tim Jessell

A
LITTLE APPLE
PAPERBACK

SCHOLASTIC INC.
New York Toronto London Auckland Sydney
Mexico City New Delhi Hong Kong Buenos Aires

Book design by Dawn Adelman

ISBN 0-439-42080-6

Text copyright © 2003 by Robert T. Abbott
Illustrations copyright © 2003 by Scholastic Inc.

All rights reserved. Published by Scholastic Inc.
SCHOLASTIC, LITTLE APPLE, and associated logos
are trademarks and/or registered trademarks of Scholastic Inc.

12 11   8/0

Printed in the U.S.A.   40
First printing, July 2003

For Katie O'Connell, Emily Sayer, Anya Hudyncia,
J. D. Eisengrein, Stephen Adams, Meghan Wells,
and all "Droonlings" here, there, and everywhere

Contents

One

A Matter of Time

"How much time do we have?" asked Eric Hinkle as he wheeled his bicycle to the front of the public library.

Julie Rubin hopped off her bike and raced up the steps. "Two hours. Neal's supposed to get us a worktable." She pushed through the doors.

Eric paused on the steps. The three friends were meeting at the library to work on school projects. They each had to create a family tree and write a report on a distant ancestor.

Eric looked out over the busy center of their little town. He smiled to himself. People were shopping, strolling, and walking their dogs.

The town had a pizza place, a movie theater, and a skate park. It was everything a town should be.

And soon it would be even better.

He looked up at the banner over Main Street:

NEW CHILDREN'S LIBRARY
GRAND OPENING PARTY AT NOON TODAY

"More books!" he cheered as he went in.

To the left of the main room were the glass doors of the new children's wing — two floors of books, computers, videos, and reading areas.

"Hey, guys," said Neal Kroger, dumping a pile of books on a nearby table. "Now, don't get me wrong. I love the library. My mom even runs the place. And making a family tree sounds fun. But I'm not a real fan of weekend homework."

Julie laughed. "It's our own fault. After our last big adventure *you know where,* we totally fell asleep in class. And missed the assignment!"

Eric smiled again.

You know where was as different from their town as any two places could possibly be.

You know where was the world of Droon, the very secret and very mysterious land Eric and his friends had discovered under his house.

It all started when a magical rainbow-colored staircase appeared in a small closet in Eric's basement. At the bottom of those stairs lay a land of mystery and adventure. And awesome friends.

Princess Keeah was a junior wizard and one of their best friends. Galen Longbeard was a master wizard of great age and power. Max was a funny orange-haired spider troll. Together, they all helped keep Droon free from the clutches of a very wicked and very powerful sorcerer. A sorcerer with fins behind his ears and a V-shaped scar on his head. A sorcerer named Lord Sparr.

The kids had helped change Droon's destiny. But Droon had changed them, too.

For one thing, Eric had gained his own wizard powers. And ever since Julie was scratched by a wingwolf, she had been able to fly. Sometimes, she could even change shape.

"Speaking of *you know where*," said Eric as he pulled a notebook from his backpack, "I keep remembering what Keeah said once. That our two worlds are tied closely together."

"That's for sure," said Julie. "Especially now that Sparr is actually here in our world."

Eric shivered. Sparr *was* in the Upper World.

In his quest for a mysterious object called the Coiled Viper, the sorcerer discovered a long-forgotten second stairway between Droon and the Upper World. It was called the Dark Stair.

"Sparr may be *here*," said Neal, "but he's not exactly *now*, if you know what I mean."

This was true, too. Blasting his way up the Dark Stair in a storm of red lightning, Sparr discovered to his astonishment that the stair led not to the present but to the past.

The year 1470, to be exact.

Sparr tried to use a time portal to travel to the present, where he knew the Viper lay hidden. But the portal collapsed.

Sparr was trapped in the past.

Julie set a yellow pad on the table and pulled two pencils from the pocket of her shorts. "I'm glad Sparr is stuck far back in time. Can you imagine if he actually came here? I mean — yikes!"

Eric breathed in deeply.

That was exactly what Sparr wanted to do.

When Keeah was four years old, she and a witch named Demither secretly climbed the rainbow stairs to Eric's house. Together, they flew out from his attic and hid something in his town.

It didn't take a wizard to guess that what they hid and what Sparr was looking for were the same thing.

The Coiled Viper.

But that wasn't the only problem. A nasty spirit named Om had once made a prophecy to Eric.

You will find it . . . and give it to Sparr.

Eric trembled to recall those words. He hoped they weren't true. He hated the idea that he would ever help someone as evil as Sparr.

"Hello, kids!" said a woman in a blue dress, coming to their table with a pile of newspapers. It was the librarian, Mrs. Kroger, Neal's mother. "I have those newspapers you wanted, Julie. They're very old, so please be careful."

"I will be. Thanks!" said Julie. "One of my ancestors was a reporter during the Civil War. I'm going to read her stories in these old papers."

"Family trees are full of interesting branches," Mrs. Kroger said, heading back to her desk.

"Interesting and sometimes strange," Neal whispered. "My aunt races motorcycles. And Grandma Kroger makes art out of old junk!"

Julie laughed. "Are you writing about them?"

"Nope," said Neal. "I'm going all the way back to 1620, to see if any of my ancestors came on the *Mayflower*, the boat the Pilgrims sailed to America."

"It's called a ship, not a boat," said Julie.

Eric grinned. "Well, I lucked out. My mom said my great-great-great-grandfather helped the Wright brothers test their airplane in 1904. The library has an old silent movie of the flight."

"Librarians love silent movies," said Neal with a chuckle.

As Julie carefully turned the pages of one old newspaper and Neal cracked open a book about the *Mayflower*, Eric went to the video shelves.

Families are pretty strange, he thought.

Not only did the powerful sea witch Demither turn out to be Keeah's aunt, but when the kids followed Sparr up the Dark Stair, they discovered that Galen and Sparr were *brothers*.

Besides that, they were both born in the Upper World and had a third brother named Urik. Urik was a wizard who helped the kids, then took off after Sparr in the time portal. Urik was trapped somewhere in time, too.

"Galen, Urik, and Sparr — brothers," Eric said as he searched. "Who would believe it —"

He stopped. There was a sudden jangle of bells and what sounded like a whisper.

"Sparr-r-r-r!"

Eric froze. He looked through the shelf. No one was there. Then he laughed. "Okay, too much thinking about Sparr!"

He found the tape he was looking for, then headed to a video workstation across the room from where Neal and Julie were reading.

He inserted the tape, forwarded to the part his mother had told him about, and pressed PLAY. The scratchy images of a silent film came on. The scene showed grassy sand dunes where a small crowd of people had gathered.

In the center stood a flimsy airplane, with wings that looked as if they were made of paper.

The propellers began to turn, and the plane moved along the ground. A man waving a white hat ran alongside the plane until a flash of light streaked across the film and the scene ended.

"That was him!" said Eric. "Mom said my great-great-great-grandfather always wore a white hat! Cool. I've got to write about him!"

Suddenly, Neal jumped up from his table. "Holy freak-out! I hope I'm not related to *him*!"

Mrs. Kroger frowned at him. "Neal, shhh."

Eric rushed over. "Neal, what is it?"

Neal pointed to the open book on the table. In it was an old ink drawing of the *Mayflower* being tossed in a storm. On the deck, barely visible in the shadows, was the crouching figure of a man. He seemed normal, except for one thing.

"Fins!" said Neal. "Look at him. He's got fins behind his ears. You know who has fins behind his ears? *Sparr* has fins behind his ears."

"It can't be," said Eric, squinting at the

book. "It's just an old picture. Julie, take a look —"

"Shhh, and listen to this!" she said, tapping her newspaper. "In 1863, in the middle of the Civil War, during a balloon flight, there's suddenly a storm of — are you ready? — red lightning!"

Neal's eyes went wide. "Red lightning? You know who likes red lightning? Sparr does!"

"No way," said Eric. "We must all have Sparr on the brain. It doesn't mean anything."

"Well, it's freaking me out," grumbled Neal.

Eric shook his head. "Let's just keep working." He walked back over to his video station, rewound the tape, and pressed PLAY again.

This time as he watched the man in the hat, he couldn't help noticing another man moving along the crowd behind the plane.

Eric's heart fluttered for a moment.

Just before the film ended, the man turned to the camera. He had deep-set eyes, a sharp nose, and a pointed beard. He also had a mark on his forehead. It looked like a scar.

A V-shaped scar.

"No way! No way!"

Eric hit the PAUSE button on the video player. His heart seemed to pause, too.

He wanted to scream but couldn't.

Finally, he just pointed at the screen.

"Guys, get over here! It's him! It's — Sparr!"

Two

Glemf?

Eric's heart was thumping like a drum as he and his friends stared at the video monitor.

"I don't believe it," whispered Julie.

"Neither do I," said Eric. "It's crazy. But it's all here in black and white. First, there's a guy on a ship in 1620. He looks a little like Sparr, but maybe it's just a bad picture. Then, in 1863, there's a storm of red lightning, Sparr's favorite kind. Finally, in 1904, there's a guy with a V-shaped scar. No one has a scar like that —"

"But it can't be Sparr," said Julie. "The time portal collapsed. Sparr was trapped in the past."

"Then what does this mean?" asked Neal.

Eric breathed in deeply. "I think it means that Sparr isn't trapped anymore. I think it means he's traveling through time. From 1470 to 1620 to 1863 to 1904. Sparr's getting closer. He's coming here. For the Viper."

"*Sparr-r-r-r!*"

Eric jumped. "That voice! I heard it earlier!"

He looked up to see a green creature about a foot tall standing on the top bookshelf. It was dressed in a red cape trimmed with tiny bells.

Eric's mouth dropped open. "What —"

The creature's big yellow eyes bulged at him.

"It's — him!" it said. "I must — glemf! — tell the others!" With that, the creature sprang to the floor and tore away between the stacks.

"Was that a frog?" asked Neal.

"A frog that said 'Sparr'?" asked Julie.

Eric blinked. "It *was* a frog that said 'Sparr.' And it's getting away! After it!"

They raced between the stacks, past the new children's room, and into the magazine area, where several patrons were reading quietly.

"There it is!" said Neal, pointing up.

Using its large webbed feet, the creature scampered straight up the wall. At the top, it turned, said "glemf," then popped out a window.

Julie started for the wall. "I'll fly up —"

"No!" said Eric. "We can't give ourselves away. Let's go outside."

They pushed open the doors just in time to see a little red cape zip under the library banner over Main Street.

"It's moving so fast, I don't think anyone sees it," said Julie.

"Probably a good thing," said Neal. "Uh-oh!"

Beeeeep! A minivan screeched to a halt as the creature sprang in front of it, then to the curb.

"Hey, keep your dog on a leash," the driver called out. "Wait — *is* it a dog?"

"Yes, sir!" said Eric. "Um . . . heel, boy!"

But the creature didn't heel. It leaped over a trash can and zigzagged among the shoppers on Main Street.

"Time to split up," said Julie. "I'll fly over the supermarket and surprise it when

it gets to the corner." She checked to see if anyone was looking, then glided up from the ground.

Eric nodded. "And if it puts up a fight, I'll stop it with a spray of blue sparks!"

Neal shrugged. "Since I don't have any powers, I'll just — run!" He cut straight across the town park, leaping over benches and sidestepping baby strollers.

As Eric ran, he felt his hands get warm. He held them up and saw tiny blue sparks springing off his fingertips. "Yeah, I may need this."

"Eric! Neal!" Julie shouted from the supermarket roof. "It went between the pizza place and the cleaners. There's no way out."

"I'm there!" said Neal, pouring on the speed.

"Ha! We've got it!" Eric tore around the

restaurant just as Julie fluttered to the ground.

Neal was already in the alley, standing in the middle of three high brick walls, staring ahead.

His mouth was open, his eyes were gaping.

"Don't tell me you lost it?" asked Julie.

"I didn't lose it," Neal said. "Well, not exactly. I mean, I saw where it went."

"Then let's follow it," said Eric.

"We can't," said Neal. "It went there."

"*There?*" Julie looked where Neal was pointing. "What do you mean? There's just *air* there."

"And that's where it went!" said Neal. "I mean, I was really zooming. I was just about to grab its little red cape, when all of a sudden — *slorp* — it's gone!"

Julie squinted at Neal. "*Slorp?* That's it?"

He nodded. "Except for the music."

Eric felt chills trickle up the back of his neck. "Music? What kind of music?"

"A weird little tune," said Neal. "Played on some kind of flute or something. Then . . . *slorp*."

Eric looked around the alley again, then down Main Street at all the people and cars and shops. Ten minutes earlier it had looked so normal.

"Something very weird is going on," he said, taking a deep breath. "First, we find out that maybe Sparr is moving through time —"

"Which is scary enough," said Julie.

Eric nodded. "Then this little green guy whispers about Sparr —"

"And vanishes with a *slorp*," added Neal.

"It's weird, all right," said Julie. "I say

we need help. The Galen and Keeah sort of help."

Eric smiled. "Then what are we waiting for?"

Five minutes later, they were tramping down to Eric's basement. Pulling aside two cartons, they entered the small closet, shut the door, switched off the light, and stood in the dark.

But not for long.

Whoosh! A rainbow-colored glow shone from beneath their feet, and they found themselves standing on the top step of a staircase circling down and away from Eric's house.

Below them was the hazy pink sky of Droon in the morning. As they stepped down, the mists began to clear, and they saw where they were.

"I see a beach," said Julie. "A small boat

is moored in the water. Look, there's Galen!"

Below them, three figures were hurrying across the beach to a thick grove of trees. In the lead was a tall bearded man in a long blue robe. He pointed to a range of cliffs dotted with caves.

"I see orange hair and lots of legs," said Neal. "Max is there, too."

"And Keeah!" said Eric, waving at a girl wearing a blue tunic and a gold crown.

But as the stairs faded and the kids ran to their friends, the waves crashed, and the surface of the sea burst open violently — *ka-whoom*!

Everyone turned. A large red hull emerged from the waves and splashed toward the shore.

Keeah stared at the water. "Oh, no!"

"Our fears have come true," said Galen.

"It's a boat!" said Neal.

"More like a ship," chirped Max.

"A big red ship," added Julie.

"Boat, ship. It's not the *Mayflower*!" said Neal.

A moment later — *fwing-ing-ing!* — streaks of fire shot from the deck and across the beach.

"Flaming arrows!" cried Eric. "It's a big red ship full of big red Ninns! Everyone take cover!"

Three

Battle on the Beach

Errrk! A hatch on the side of the ship opened, and dozens of Sparr's red warriors plopped onto the sand. "We see you! We get you!" they cried.

"To the caves!" said Galen, already starting to run. "Max, spin us a rope, if you please."

"At once, master!" Max's eight furry legs blurred into action, weaving a stout rope of the finest spider silk. When they got to the cliff, he threw it up to the entrance of a large cave.

"Up we go!" cheered the spider troll.

When they reached the cave, Galen turned. "Keeah, how about something special for our charming friends down there?"

"I don't mind if I do!" said the princess. Smiling, she raised her hand, and a swirl of blue sparks streamed down to the trees below.

Suddenly, the branches came alive, twisting and turning and grabbing the Ninns as they charged up the sand.

"That should slow them down!" chirped Max.

Galen turned to Eric and his friends. "Sparr's warriors rarely sail this close to Jaffa City. They must know our secret."

"What secret?" asked Julie.

"The reason we are here," said Keeah. "We came to hide the Eye of the Viper in the cliffs."

While Galen stood guard like a mighty oak tree over the cave entrance, Max opened a pouch on his belt and removed a small box.

He gave it to Princess Keeah.

Unclasping the lock, she lifted the lid. Nestled in deep folds of red velvet lay a small blue jewel.

"The Eye of the Viper," gasped Eric.

Even in the cave's dim light, the gem seemed to glow with inner life. It was one of two twin eyes meant for the mysterious Coiled Viper.

"Keeah, tell our friends what you discovered."

The princess nodded at Galen. "I spent some time studying it and figured out it's the right eye. And look here." She pointed to a shiny fleck glimmering on the back of the gem.

Neal leaned in for a closer look. "It looks like gold. But it's different from regular gold."

"It is red gold," said Galen, smiling at Neal. "The rarest and most mystical of Droon's five golds. Luckily, Sparr is trapped far in the past, or he would try to steal back the Eye himself."

Eric looked at his friends, then at the wizard. "That's sort of why we came here. We're pretty sure Sparr isn't so far in the past anymore."

Taking turns, the kids told what they had discovered at the library and how the strange green creature had spoken Sparr's name.

"Ah-yaaa!" A sudden cry rose from the beach.

"Oh, no," chittered Max. "The Ninns are free!"

Looking grim, Galen strode to the back of the cave and touched what looked like a solid wall. It slid open, revealing a passage that turned downward, into the mountain.

"If Sparr has found a way through time," he said, "then he comes for the Viper. All the more important to hide the Eye. Max, put it back in your pouch. Everyone, follow me!"

As they followed Galen into the passage, Eric could tell they were all thinking the same thing.

What exactly is the Coiled Viper?

Even as they journeyed deeper into the mountain, Galen spoke as if he heard their thoughts.

"I do not know what the Coiled Viper is. Even after Sparr created it, even after I stole it and hid it, I never saw its true shape."

"It must be very powerful," said Keeah.

"Unimaginably powerful," he said. "I know of only one object whose power might rival it."

"Can we use it against Sparr?" asked Julie.

The wizard shook his head. "Alas, it was lost with Urik in the past of your world. It was a stone of pure white called the Moon Medallion. My mother, Queen Zara, inscribed it with a mystical poem that held great power over our family. But the Viper's magic is darker and older still. That is why I hid it away."

"Too bad the Viper didn't stay hidden," said Neal.

"Quite right," said Max. "It changed shape again and again until Witch Demither found it."

Keeah nodded as they entered a series

of rough tunnels. "Then Demither took me with her to your world to hide the Viper. I keep trying to remember more about where it might be, but it was so long ago."

"Maybe it should just stay hidden," said Eric.

Galen stopped and turned. "Eric, I know what you fear. That the spirit Om's words will come true. That you will give the Viper to Sparr."

Eric nodded.

The wizard smiled. "Urik comes from the same long line of wizards that I come from. And he always said that greatness comes to us when we need it most."

"I come from a pretty short line — just me!"

Galen laughed. "That may just be enough."

Boom-oom-oom! The passage shook.

Rocks fell from the ceiling, showering them with dust.

"The Ninns are firing at us from the ship!" cried Max. "We must hurry along."

Boom-oom-oom! Suddenly, a chunk of wall crumbled before them, and daylight streaked across the passage. An instant later, a small army of Ninns squeezed into the tunnel.

"Give me the Eye!" the chief Ninn demanded.

"I don't think so!" cried Keeah. Together, she, Galen, and Eric sent a blast at the Ninns. But the red warriors jerked their shields up, and the sparks bounced back at the children. In a flash, the Ninns overpowered Max, tearing from his belt the pouch that held the Eye of the Viper. Then they dashed back out the hole.

Boom-oom-oom! Another blast from

the ship sealed the wizard and the children in the tunnel.

By the time Galen blew a passage through the rocks, the Ninns were back on the ship.

"Set sail to Kano!" cheered the red warriors.

Kano was at the center of Sparr's Dark Lands and the home of his towering volcano palace.

Max raced to the shore, shaking his furry fists at the ship. "Going to Kano, are you?" he cried. "We'll follow you! We'll take back our jewel!"

Galen joined his friend on the sand. "Well said, Max. We *shall* take it back."

He pulled back his robe to reveal a curved fighting staff hanging from his belt.

"Friends," he said, turning to the children, "we must fight our battle on two fronts. Max and I will follow the Ninns. If

Sparr is traveling through time for the Viper itself, you must go to the Upper World to stop him. It may even mean finding the Viper yourselves."

"What about our little froggy guy?" said Neal.

Keeah smiled. "When something vanishes, it usually goes somewhere. The clue is in that alley."

With a flourish, Galen raised up his hand. A light rose from his palm and flashed across the air. The stairs shimmered into view before them.

"Farewell, friends," said Max. "Good luck!"

Waving, the wizard and the spider troll set off in their small boat. Though little, it seemed to speed magically over the waves, following the Ninn ship.

The children quickly climbed the rainbow stairs. At the top, they carefully stepped out into the basement. It was just as they'd left it.

Keeah looked around. "I wish I could remember where the Viper lies hidden."

"Let's go to the attic," said Julie. "You flew over the town from there. Maybe you'll remember something."

"Good idea," said Eric.

Up through the kitchen and living room they went, past Eric's room, and up the attic stairs.

Moving aside a box of Christmas decorations, Eric slowly opened the attic window.

Keeah looked out, a breeze stirring her hair.

"It's different," she whispered. "Or I'm different. It was so long ago, I don't see . . . anything . . . familiar. Oh!"

Her eyes closed. She wobbled on her feet.

"Do you remember something?" asked Julie.

"Seven trees . . . in a circle," Keeah said. Then she blinked. "That's all I remember."

Kkkkk! Suddenly, the air crackled, and a bright red streak of light zigzagged across the sky.

"Red lightning!" said Julie.

"It landed near the pizza place!" said Neal. "In the alley, right where we saw the green guy!"

Seconds later, they heard a sound. *Slorp-p-p!*

Eric felt his knees go weak. He looked at his friends. He knew what the lightning meant. He wanted to yell, but all he could do was whisper.

"It's — it's — Sparr. He's — here!"

Four

Play It Again, Neal!

Eric stared out the window, shivering. "Sparr is here. The Coiled Viper is here. It's all happening just like Om said it would. I can't believe it."

Keeah shook her head. "Eric, we'll make sure Sparr never gets his hands on the Viper."

"You bet he won't," said Julie. "Sparr's messing on our turf now. We're the home team."

"Yeah," said Neal. "I say, let's bust him good!"

Eric looked at his friends. It felt good to have them there. And it was true. They were a team.

The best team ever.

"Okay, then," he said, taking a deep breath and starting down the stairs, "the longer we wait, the more time Sparr has to do his nasty work. The clue is in that alley. Let's go!"

They rushed downstairs.

Squeak!

They stopped. The kitchen door opened, and footsteps crossed the floor.

"Oh, no!" said Julie. "Your parents! Keeah, your clothes, your crown!"

"What's wrong?" asked the princess.

Neal made a face. "Nothing, except that we don't have too many princesses in this town!"

"We'll pretend you're a new girl," Eric whispered. "It'll be okay. Just play it cool."

The kids entered the kitchen. Mr. and Mrs. Hinkle seemed surprised to see Keeah.

"Hello," they said together.

Before she caught herself, Keeah started to make a deep bow. "Hello. I am honored and very pleased to meet the parents of such a —"

"This is Keeah!" Eric interrupted. "Just plain old Keeah . . . Smith! She's new in town, and we're showing her around."

"We started in the attic!" Neal blurted out. "And now we're in the kitchen. See the kitchen, Keeah? It's where people cook."

Julie gave him a nudge. "Neal, you're freaking out. Just calm down."

Neal scowled. "You sound like my mom."

Eric's parents looked at Neal, then at Julie, then at Eric, and finally at Keeah's blue tunic and the crown shining on her head.

"Is that crown made of real gold?" asked Mrs. Hinkle.

"She was in a play," said Eric.

"Cinderella!" said Julie.

"And the Seven Dwarfs!" added Neal.

"Sounds . . . interesting," said Mrs. Hinkle.

"And speaking of costumes," said Neal, "have you seen anyone all in black, with red fins growing from his ears? I mean, fake fins, obviously?"

Mr. Hinkle's eyebrows went up. "Fins?"

"And a big V-shaped scar," said Neal.

"Also fake," said Julie. "Because, like, who would have real red fins and a V-shaped scar?"

"So, have you seen him?" asked Eric.

His parents glanced at each other. "Not

recently," said Mr. Hinkle. "But if we go to the library party, maybe we'll see him later."

With that, Mr. and Mrs. Hinkle excused themselves and went into the living room.

Eric turned to his friends. "That's what I'm afraid of. That *everyone* will see Sparr later."

"Unless we stop him first," said Julie. "Come on, Keeah. Let's get you dressed to blend in."

They rushed across the street to Julie's house.

Ten minutes later, Keeah was dressed in blue jeans, a green T-shirt, and sneakers. Her tunic and crown were stuffed into a small cloth bag with a big flower on it.

"Great," said Neal. "But lighten up on the bowing and the princess talk. You're making us look bad."

"Got it, dude!" she said.

Eric laughed. "Okay, now. To the alley."

On the way, the kids told Keeah every detail about how they had chased the strange green creature between the buildings and how it had vanished into thin air. When they arrived at the alley, the pavement had a red streak across it.

"That's where the lightning struck," said Keeah. "This must be the place."

"That's just it," said Eric, running his hands along the rough brick walls. "The place for what? There are no doors, no windows. The walls are thick and old. Where did Mr. Froggy — and Sparr — go?"

"What's this?" asked Julie, bending down to pick up a small, curved tube of wood with a series of tiny holes running down the length of it.

Neal gasped. "That must be the flute thingy the green guy played just before it vanished!"

Keeah looked at it. "There are some people in Droon whose music has magical powers. Neal, do you remember how the song went?"

"I don't think I'll ever forget it," he said. "Let me see if I can figure out how to play it."

He took the little flute, placed his fingers over the holes, and raised it to his lips. He squeezed his eyes shut, took a breath, and blew into the flute, lifting his fingers one by one.

Weee-ooo-e-o-e-o-e-ooo! What came out was the most mysterious sound the children had ever heard. It sounded like wind whistling in the trees, or owls hooting, or water burbling over rocks in a stream, or all three combined.

"You are good at that," said Julie.

Neal opened his eyes, grinning. "I never knew I could play like . . . like . . . whoa!"

All at once, the air in front of them began to ripple like the surface of a pond into which a pebble has been dropped.

Staring into it, they couldn't see the rough brick walls of the alley anymore.

As if they were looking through a waterfall, they could just make out what appeared to be a street curving away from where they stood.

And trees in the distance. And a range of hills.

"Ummm," said Eric, then stopped.

"I agree," said Julie.

"Let me guess," said Keeah, staring ahead. "You haven't been to this neighborhood before?"

Neal shook his head. "Pretty much not."

They stood there, staring at the wobbling air.

"We should go in," said Keeah.

"Yeah," said Eric. "Definitely. I mean, it's probably where that little green guy went. And unless Sparr is having a slice at the pizza place, that's probably where he went, too."

"So what are we waiting for?" asked Julie.

"Give me a second," said Neal. "I'll come up with something. Got it! Let's just grab a few doughnuts from that place way across town, then we'll go in. I know the way, come on!"

Keeah grabbed Neal by the arm. "No more stalling. Sparr's in there. We need to go in. If nobody wants to lead, we'll go in together."

So the four friends pushed slowly, carefully, and very close together, right through the wall of rippling air.

Five

Beyond the Veil

S-l-l-l-o-r-r-p-p-p!

When they stepped through, Eric felt for an instant as if he were suddenly soaking wet, then not. It was like they had somehow passed through a wall of slithering, sliding water but had come out the other side completely dry.

"Well, that was the weirdest thing," said Julie, looking down at her clothes.

Slipping the flute into his pocket, Neal

whispered, "Can you believe what we're looking at?"

"Not really, no," said Eric.

Before them, as far as the eye could see, were tents. Hundreds of tents, of every color and size, pitched along the narrow, winding street ahead of them and far up the sides of every hill.

And the air was filled with the strange, haunting music of flutes and horns and bells.

"It's beautiful in a way," said Keeah.

"It's as if," said Eric, struggling to put it into words, "as if this is what our town might look like without the buildings."

"The sky is different," said Neal.

This was true. For while the sun had been shining in their town, the sky above them now was a dark swirl of smoke and clouds. And the vast gray sea heaving in the distance looked as if a storm might strike any second.

"I can see why Sparr would like it here," said Julie. "It's dark enough."

"And cold enough," said Keeah, rubbing her hands. "Let's keep going. Carefully now."

As they stepped farther along the street, they passed under a kind of gate made of wood and draped with brightly colored cloths and banners.

Looking up, Eric saw a single word carved into the top of the gate: CALIBAZ.

"So," he said, "I guess we're in Calibaz."

"Wherever that is," mumbled Julie.

With each step they took, the music seemed to get louder and closer.

Then suddenly — *thomp, thomp!* — the ground thundered behind them.

"Someone's coming! Hide!" said Keeah.

She whirled around, lifted the flap of a small tent, and pulled everyone in.

After making sure they were alone, the kids crouched down, lifted the flap, and looked out.

Stomping down the narrow street was a row of big animals. They were as large as elephants and like them in many ways, except that their thick, leathery skin was blue. And instead of a trunk, each beast bore a wide, flat nose that looked like a shovel. Two enormous baskets were strapped on the back of each animal.

"Cool! The Calibaz circus!" chirped Neal.

"Froggy guys, too," whispered Julie. "Look."

Following the beasts were several green creatures like the little one they had seen earlier. They all had the same spindly frog-like bodies with big feet, and they all

sported bright capes trimmed with rows of tiny silver bells.

"It looks like a family of those beings you saw," whispered Keeah. "They must live here."

"We won't find out unless we get out there and explore," said Julie. "I say we get changed." She pointed to piles of loose cloth in the tent.

Keeah frowned. "But I really like wearing my Z-shirt."

"T-shirt!" said Eric with a laugh. "And unless it says CALIBAZ ELEMENTARY, it'll give us away."

"I guess I'll go for blue," she said.

"I claim the purple cape!" said Neal, grabbing a long violet-colored cloth and tying it around his neck. He also wound a scarf over his face.

Just as he was about to choose a color,

Eric heard a strangely familiar sound. "Glemf!"

"The froggy guy!" he said. "I hear it —"

Eric tiptoed to the back wall of the tent and peeked out between the curtains. When he did, he found himself staring nose to nose with the green creature he had seen in the library.

"It's you!" cried Eric.

"It's him!" the creature shrieked at the top of its lungs. "It's — glemf! — him!"

"Me?" Eric tried to jump back into the tent, but green hands came from everywhere at once and pulled him out.

"Yikes!" he cried. He crouched low, twisted out of their grasp, and started running full-speed down the street. "Help!"

In seconds, the street was jammed with green creatures running toward Eric, the bells on their capes jangling loudly.

The cry went up, "The boy! The boy is here!"

"What? What!" Eric yelped. "Why me?"

He tore blindly around a corner, only to come face to face with yet another mob of green creatures. He jumped back and into a side alley.

Thomp, Thomp! A giant shovel-nosed beast came lumbering down the narrow street toward him. Without thinking, Eric sprang up to one of its giant saddle baskets and crouched down inside it.

The green creatures rushed along the street toward the beast but did not look in the baskets.

Carefully, Eric peeked over the top to see what was happening. The crowd filled the street on every side. "Oh, great. I'm trapped. In Calibaz!"

Eric! Are you okay? a voice spoke in his head.

"Huh?" He peered over the sea of green faces and saw a flash of blue cloth.

Keeah? he answered back silently. Communicating without actually talking was one of the cool powers Eric and Keeah shared.

A small hand waved from beneath the cloth. Neal stood next to Keeah, completely covered in a long purple cape. Next to him was Julie, wearing a swirl of yellow-and-red stripes.

I guess I'm okay for now, Eric said to his friends. *Keep going. Try to find Sparr. I'll blast my way back to you if I have to. I promise!*

"You'd better, or I'll freak out!" yelled Neal.

Meet us at the gates, said Keeah. *If you don't, we'll turn this place upside down!*

Some joke. It's already upside down,

Eric thought as the crowd drove the big beast farther along what should have been Main Street.

Finally, the green creatures heard a noise and rushed off in another direction, leaving the beast to lumber away alone.

"Now's my chance," said Eric. He stood up and prepared to make his escape, then froze.

At the bottom of the other basket, he spied two large yellow eyes blinking up at him.

And he heard that word again.

"Glemf!"

Six

City of Tents

Eric stared at the green face.

"You!" he said. "You're the cause of all this trouble. Come out. Let me see you!"

Trembling, the creature stood, then clambered into Eric's basket. It crouched at his feet, turning its big eyes up at him.

"Well," said Eric, "who and *what* are you?"

"I'm just a hoobah," it said in a squeaky

whisper. "Pikoo is my name. Don't —
glemf! — hurt me."

Eric frowned. "Me, hurt you? It's like
you're trying to hurt me! Why is everyone
chasing me?"

Pikoo swallowed. "Lord Sparr told
us to."

Eric drew in a breath. "So it's true?
Sparr is here? Now?"

Spreading his mouth wide as if to smile
but not quite making it, Pikoo nodded.
"Sparr visited Calibaz once a long time
ago. He told our great-great-great-grand-
fathers about the boy who would help
him one day. I was so excited when I saw
you in the library!"

Eric groaned. "I won't help him! And
neither should you. He's bad. Very bad."

"He said you might say that."

Eric looked out from the basket. The

beast tramped into a narrow alley, fluttering the tent curtains on either side.

"Okay," he said, "let me get this straight. Sparr came to Calibaz in the past and told you to watch out for me. Well, I'm here now, and he's here now. But where is here? What is Calibaz?"

Pikoo's eyes seemed to twinkle. "Calibaz is the City of Tents! Where bells chime and flutes play and my people dream of hope! It lies on the other side of the veil from your world."

"I didn't even know there *was* a veil!" said Eric. "Has Calibaz always been here?"

Pikoo giggled. "Calibaz has always *been*, but never *here*. We live in tents because our city is always moving."

"What do you mean, *moving*?" asked Eric.

Pikoo turned his face to the dark sky.

"A legend says that Calibaz must move each day and night, until a stranger leads us into the world of light. Your world is the world of light."

Eric shook his head. "This is unbelievable. A city that travels around — *next* to our world?"

The tents were thinning out, and more blue beasts seemed to be moving along the street.

"Where are we going?" asked Eric.

"To the pit Sparr told us to dig," said Pikoo. "If we dig it, he said he will lead us into your world of light. He says he came here just for us. And that you will help him."

Eric looked at the hoobah's huge eyes. They were full of hope. He knew the truth would hurt, but he had to say it. "I — I — I'm sorry, Pikoo, but I don't think Sparr really came to Calibaz to help you. He came because he's searching for something called the Coiled Viper. It's hidden on our side. Once he finds it, we'll all be in real trouble."

Pikoo's eyes grew large. "But our legend —"

Thomp, thomp! The large blue beast stopped walking.

Eric poked his head over the basket and saw a giant pit, dug deep into the earth. Dozens of blue beasts were circling down a narrow pathway to the very center of the pit, while others were circling back up another road.

"The beasts' noses are good for shoveling," Pikoo said as their animal started tramping into the pit.

Shoveling? thought Eric. *What is Sparr up to?*

When their beast reached the bottom, Eric and Pikoo jumped out of the basket.

The creature then stooped to the earth and drove its nose into the ground, pulling up a big snoutful of dirt. It tilted its head back, and the dirt slid off into the saddle baskets, filling them.

As it did, a stream of black smoke drifted up from the center of the hole, adding to the darkness in the air.

"This is crazy," Eric said. "What is all this?"

He edged toward the hole. Waving aside the smoke, he peered down. Below the hole was a mass of black rock, glowing red in the center with smoke pouring up from it in thick black plumes.

Pikoo leaned over. "What do you see?"

It finally struck Eric what he was looking at.

The smoldering tip of a volcano.

"It can't be," he gasped. "Is that Kano?

That's — that's Droon down there! I can't believe it. Sparr made you dig all the way to Droon!"

Eric jumped back. Something small and red poked up from the hole. It wiggled around. Soon, the one red thing was joined by five others just like it.

Claws.

Six claws on a hand.

The hand of a Ninn.

"Holy cow!" Eric gasped. He grabbed Pikoo and jumped behind a mound of dirt. First one, then another, then a third Ninn climbed out of the hole, shook themselves, looked around, and growled at the sound of music in the air.

Moments later, Eric heard clanging weapons and thumping war drums as more and more Ninns jammed themselves up through the hole.

"Now we find Sparr!" cried one of the Ninns. Together, they trudged up the pit, drumming loudly to drown out the hoobah music.

"Sparr's army of Ninns is here!" said Eric. "That's why they traveled to Kano. To get up here. To help Sparr steal the Viper!"

"So he doesn't plan to help us?" Pikoo said.

Eric's heart was racing. "Sorry, Pikoo. Sparr only helps himself — to Droon, to our world, and now he's helped himself to Calibaz, too. I need to find my friends and stop Sparr from finding the Viper."

Pikoo scowled as more Ninns drummed their way up the pit and into the city of tents.

"Even if our legend doesn't come true today," he said, "it isn't the end of our world. There is still hope for tomorrow. I will call the hoobahs and tell them to help you!"

"You would do that?"

Pikoo smiled and started up the pit. "Of course! Find your friends. Then follow the smell of burning wood. It will lead you to the tent of Sparr. You can't miss it. Ours are colorful. His is very big, very black, and very ugly. Good luck!"

Then Pikoo took a little horn from his cape and began to play. A moment later, hoobahs from around the city answered on their flutes.

His heart pounding, Eric darted off into the city of tents to search for his friends.

Seven

A Face from Far Away

While Ninns stormed along the narrow streets as if they owned the city, Eric dashed from tent to tent, careful to keep from being seen.

Five minutes later, he saw three figures huddled near the wooden gate. One of them had a silly purple cape pulled over his head.

"Neal!" he said, laughing as he ran over.

Neal turned. "Eric! Boy, are we glad to see you. I almost freaked out!"

"What happened to you?" asked Keeah, quickly wrapping Eric in an orange robe and hood.

"We were looking and looking," said Julie. "Then, suddenly, there were Ninns everywhere!"

"Um, yeah, about that." As quickly as he could, Eric told them everything he had learned, including Pikoo's description of Sparr's tent.

"We passed a big black tent," said Keeah.

"And it was ugly and scary," said Julie.

"Sounds like the place," said Eric. "Let's go."

They twisted through the streets until they found the tent of black cloth. The air was thicker and smokier than anywhere else in the city.

"Sparr's got a great sense of style," whispered Neal. "Somewhere between icky and yucky."

Looking both ways, the four friends slipped into a twisting maze of curtained alleys until only a single thin curtain remained between them and the innermost chamber of the tent.

Suddenly — *whoomf!* — a dazzling green-and-blue flame shot up from a cauldron inside the chamber, lighting it for an instant.

And they saw him.

In a chair against the back wall sat the great sorcerer himself, silent and unmoving.

"He's — different," Keeah whispered.

Sparr's famous black cloak was in shreds. His left arm was held close to his body, as if it were hurt. And the V-shaped scar on his head blazed more brightly and seemed deeper than ever.

"I guess his ride through time was a bit bumpy," said Neal.

"Not bumpy enough," whispered Julie. "He made it this far."

"Arise," said Sparr, lifting his hand.

Whoomf! A second rush of flames shot up from the cauldron, rustling the curtains.

"You have called me again?" asked a deep, eerie voice.

Keeah trembled, even as she tugged the curtain aside and looked in. "That voice . . ."

Sparr rose from the chair, wincing in pain as he hobbled to the cauldron. The moment he came near, white smoke rose from the fire.

And out of the smoke a face began to form.

It was a woman with wild green hair.

Her skin was pale white, her lips were black. The flames leaped around her, then settled down again.

Keeah began to shake. "Oh, my gosh! It's Witch Demither!"

Unaware of the four friends behind the curtain, Sparr stared directly at the face of smoke. "I have journeyed five centuries to find the Viper. From one time portal to the next. I was hurt."

"Not enough," hissed Neal.

"I have arrived at the right time and place," Sparr said. "You hid the Viper here."

"You may have power over me, Sparr," she said, "but I will not tell you where."

Sparr grinned coldly. "It doesn't matter. Om predicted that it will be mine anyway. But that is just the beginning. There is another problem."

Wincing in pain, Sparr pulled up a chain

that hung around his neck. On it was a pale white stone, carved all over with strange markings.

Eric felt his heart skip a beat. "Is that — that's not the medallion Galen was telling us about?"

"Where did you find that?" asked Demither.

"In the past," said the sorcerer. "Here in the Upper World. I fought someone. I took it. I must know what the markings mean."

The white stone flashed in the flame's light. Eric staggered, as if he had been struck. "It *is* the Moon Medallion! He stole it from Urik!"

Her face floating in the smoke, her eyes glistening like black jewels, Demither began to read the carvings on the stone.

"'One rides swiftly through an ancient forest. He seeks a dark goal.'"

"I am the rider," said Sparr. "I seek the Viper, and much beyond that."

"'The rider strays from the path. A branch of the tree strikes him down. He falls —'"

"A branch of the tree strikes me down?" cried Sparr. "Galen! I knew it."

Demither held up a scaly hand. "'He falls — unless that branch is broken before he enters the forest. Unless . . . that branch is broken now!'"

Sparr drew in a long breath, saying nothing for a long while. Finally, he spoke.

"And can this medallion help me?"

Demither was silent for a time, too. "It holds great power over the sons of Zara. Power for good *or* evil. How will you use it?"

"I know how," hissed Keeah. "Against Galen."

Even in his pain, Sparr managed a smile. He tucked the medallion back into his robes. "Very well, then. If I must break the branch, I shall. Go back to Droon. Await my —"

Whoomf! Demither was gone before he finished. Sparr glared at the flames. Then he turned. "Ninns!" he called out. "Ninns!"

The kids ducked between two curtains as several Ninns entered the innermost room.

"Is my army ready?" Sparr asked.

The Ninns bowed. "Yes, Lord Sparr!"

"And the Viper's Eye. Do you have it?"

The Ninns hung their heads. "The old one with the beard and the spider followed us to Kano. They stole it back."

"What?" cried Sparr.

"YESSS!" Eric shouted, punching his fist

into the air and accidentally pulling down the curtain he and his friends were hiding behind.

Sparr whirled around and stared at them, his eyes huge.

"Y-y-y-you!" he sputtered.

Eric gulped. "We'll just be leaving now."

"Get them!" Sparr howled.

Blam, blam! Keeah grabbed her friends and was already blasting a path through the tent.

The Ninns shot after them, tearing through the tent and on to the street.

Only seconds ahead of them, the kids zigzagged from one alley to another until they screeched to a stop in front of the Calibaz gate.

"Play it, Neal!" said Julie. "Play it now!"

Neal tore the little flute out of his pocket.

As the Ninns stormed around the corner toward them, he lifted it to his lips.

"Hurry," Keeah urged him.

Neal put his fingers over the holes. He took a deep breath. He paused. He let out his breath.

"I forget the tune."

Eric jumped. "You — *what?*"

The Ninns were speeding toward them.

"You know how sometimes you have a song in your head and you can't get rid of it and it keeps playing over and over in your mind and nothing you do will get it out of your head?"

The Ninns drew their bows.

Eric nodded frantically. "Yeah, so?"

"Well, this isn't like that," said Neal. "Not a bit. My mind just went totally blank."

"You said you'd never forget that tune!" said Julie.

With their arrows loaded, the Ninns charged.

"Apparently," said Neal, "I was wrong."

"NEEEEEEAL!" cried Keeah. "PLAY IT!"

"Okay, *now* you're just freaking me out!"

✸ Eight ✸

Hidden . . . and Waiting

Fwing-ing-ing! The Ninns loosed their flaming arrows at the kids.

Neal closed his eyes. "Oh, wait a second."

"A second!" cried Eric. "In a second we'll —"

Neal blew into the flute.

The strange melody filled the air, then made it wobble and ripple and — *s-s-s-l-o-r-p!* — the kids fell through to the other side. The instant Neal stopped playing, the air sealed up again.

Clank! Clonk! Blimf! The Ninns' arrows struck the wall of air on the other side, and a moment later, so did they. "Ooof! Argh! Yeow!"

"Neal!" cried Julie. "Way to keep us waiting until the last second!"

He grinned. "Yeah, I am pretty awesome, when you think about it. You're welcome!"

Eric looked down Main Street in both directions. People were everywhere. "Look, we only have a few minutes before Sparr busts his way out of Calibaz for the Viper. Keeah —"

The princess was trembling. Her eyes were closed. "I see . . . seven trees in a circle . . . a ring of trees . . . and a fountain."

Eric looked at Neal, then at Julie. "I still can't think of any place like that."

"I can!" said Julie. "I saw it this morning. In a picture of the old library. It showed a little garden of peach trees with a fountain just like that."

"There's no fountain at the library," said Eric.

Neal gasped. "Not anymore. But there was. It was right behind the library. They took it away when they built the children's library."

Keeah's eyes popped open. "Then the Viper must be hidden behind the new building. I remember Demither digging."

"Come on. We're wasting time!" said Eric.

They raced up Main Street and across the park, then stopped. A huge crowd of parents and children was lined up around the library.

Eric moaned. "Of course. It's noon.

Sparr's army will attack with the whole town here!"

"Maybe we should just force our way through and say we're sorry later?" asked Keeah.

Neal shook his head. "Only my mom could get us in, but she won't. She and the library volunteers are as tough as Ninns. No special treatment, she always says. And she's the boss."

Julie's eyes twinkled. "The boss, huh? I have an idea. We've been doing disguises all day. Time for a *real* disguise. Turn around, everyone. This may not be pretty."

When they turned around they heard the sound of rushing wind, two high-pitched squeaks, and a *ploink*! Finally, a voice said, "Follow me, children. And re-member, be quiet!"

Neal turned. Julie was now a tall

woman in a blue dress. He staggered back. "Mom?"

"Not quite," Julie said with a giggle.

"But you look just like her!" said Eric.

"I don't know for how long," she said. "Come on, everyone. And Neal, tuck in your shirt!"

"Aw, Mom!" he said.

Julie sprang up the front steps of the library, smiled at the volunteers, and led the way straight through the doors of the new children's wing, then downstairs to the ground floor.

Keeah stopped. Standing in the center of the room, she closed her eyes and began to tremble.

"Do you remember any more?" asked Eric.

"Demither was so afraid of the Viper," said Keeah. "She told me terrible things would happen if Sparr got hold of it. She couldn't fight him, but she hoped someone else could."

Eric saw fear in Keeah's face. He felt it, too. He wanted to tell her it would be okay. That everything would turn out all right.

But he couldn't. He wasn't sure it would.

The air suddenly crackled overhead.

"Lightning," said Julie. "Sparr's on his way."

Keeah turned to a story-time area filled with colorful pillows. She pointed down a short hallway to a gray metal door.

"That leads outside," said Neal.

Keeah shuddered as she walked toward the door. "It's out there."

Eric aimed a narrow stream of sparks at the door. *Zzzt!* The door popped open on to a small grassy area behind the library.

It was hedged in by a row of bushes.

Nearby were some planks of wood, a mound of dirt, and several shovels left by the library builders.

Keeah stepped out. She went three paces left, then five paces out. She looked down. "Here."

Julie transformed back into herself, and together the four friends grabbed shovels and began to dig. They dug deeper and deeper until —

Clank!

Eric tossed his shovel aside. "There's a rock blocking the way. I have to go down." Trembling, he squirmed into the hole. As soon as he did he heard Om's words screaming in his head.

You will find it!

"You just keep quiet!" he snapped.

The air in the hole was heavy and dark. Eric felt suddenly exhausted as he knelt in the dirt.

"It's powerful," said Julie. "I feel it up here."

The sound of drums thumped in the distance.

Neal peeked around the side of the library. "Ninns on Main Street," he said.

"Demither said it was a thing of darkness," said Keeah. "Be careful, Eric."

And yet as Eric heaved the rock aside, what he found was not a thing of darkness at all. Light burst up from the dirt, shining from a golden object buried there.

Eric cried out. "I have it!"

You will find it and bring it to Sparr!

He tugged the object out with both hands. It came loose from the dirt around it. Pulling himself out of the hole, he lifted the thing up for everyone to see.

Keeah gasped when she saw it. "A . . . crown! The Coiled Viper is a crown!"

It was a crown, a ring of gold, shaped

like a snake — a viper — coiled three times upon itself. Jaws wide, tongue out, fangs extended, its head was wound together with its tail and raised up.

Raised up . . . as if ready to strike.

"It's horrible," said Julie. "And beautiful."

"It's red gold," said Neal, gaping at it.

Light circled along the crown's red-tinged golden skin, making it seem alive, slithering with fiery color — green, blue, purple, black.

It surprised Eric that he could touch it at all. It felt as if it would uncoil itself and strike at him.

Did it suddenly move in his hand? Did it twist its golden head to look at him? Or was it just a trick of its own light? No, it couldn't look at him. It had no eyes. The dark holes were empty. The two blue gems would go there.

The sound of war drums filled the air.

"The Ninns are closing in," said Neal.

"Sparr, too!" said Julie. "Let's get out there."

Clutching the crown tightly, Eric raced around the library after his friends, only to find the street full of townspeople, frozen in fear.

For there was Lord Sparr, on a throne carried by a troop of Ninns, marching, marching, marching right up the center of Main Street. Sparr's fins burned a deep purple, and his eyes flashed redder than the lightning crashing overhead.

The four friends stood there, trembling.

"This is it," said Keeah.

"Sparr's really here in our world," said Eric.

"Marching up Main Street," said Julie.

Neal nodded. "Is it okay to freak out now?"

Nine

The Moon Medallion

Kkkkk! Lightning blasted over the street, sending the townspeople scattering for cover.

Eric shouted at the top of his lungs. "Run! Everyone, go home. There's going to be a —"

"A battle? I hope so!" cried Sparr, leaping from the throne. "How's this for starters?"

Blam! A spray of red sparks struck the library steps. Eric was thrown back into Julie and Neal and dropped the Coiled Viper. It let out a low, hissing noise.

Take me to Sparrrrrr!

"You be quiet!" Eric snapped, snatching up the crown and looping it on his belt.

"Give it to me!" yelled Sparr, stomping toward Eric. "It's mine. I made it. I want it. I need it!"

"Eric, together," said Keeah. They both blasted Sparr, but the evil sorcerer shot a bolt of lightning from his raised hand, and their blasts went wild.

"You should have tried that in the tent!" Sparr sneered. "I was weak then. But already I grow stronger. Soon, I shall have that crown and be stronger still. With the Viper I shall —"

"Oh, shush up!" boomed a familiar

voice. And a bolt of silvery light exploded near Sparr, wheeling him backward into a handful of Ninns.

The kids spun around. Out of the smoke came a tall man in a long blue robe, brandishing a wooden staff that shone in a rainbow of colors. Next to him ran an eight-legged spider troll.

"Galen! Max!" shouted Neal.

"Can you use a helping hand?" chirped Max, shooting a web of sticky spider silk at the Ninns. "Or should I say helping feet?"

"Yes!" said Keeah. "How did you get here?"

The old wizard hurled a second bolt at Sparr and pulled the children to safety. "We raided the Ninns, stole back the Eye, then rushed here first thing. Eric, I think your mother — sweet lady — was surprised to see us tramping out of her basement!"

Eric blinked. "She saw you?"

"I'll have to erase her memory, of course. Everyone's, actually. But first, you must take the Viper to safety. Go to Droon. King Zello and Queen Relna are waiting in Jaffa City."

Sparr leaped to his feet, his eyes flashing as he clutched the medallion around his neck.

Eric trembled. "Galen — the Moon Medallion. Sparr has it."

The wizard shot a glance a Sparr. "Ah, it gets worse! Eric, go now! Children, take him away!"

"We will," said Keeah. "You watch out."

Galen nodded. "I always do! Now, go!"

The old wizard sent blast after silver blast at Sparr, while Keeah, Neal, and Max sprang from the library steps. Eric and Julie jumped on their bikes, hotly pursued by a troop of Ninns.

The five friends raced down the street, skidding through a coffee shop, a bookstore, and a dry cleaner's before the Ninns cornered them in a yard where a family was grilling on their patio.

"Here they come!" said Julie, jumping from her bike and flying up to a nearby apple tree to look around. "Everyone, get ready!"

"Ready?" said the father at the grill. "Ready for what — ahhh!" He dropped his spatula when three big red-faced Ninns crashed into his yard.

"We're terribly sorry about this," said Keeah, taking a moment to bow to the family before pushing the first Ninn into the lawn sprinkler.

"Get the Viper!" cried the second Ninn.

"Viper?" said the mother. "But we're having hot dogs."

"Mmmm!" the third Ninn grunted as he

swept the food off the grill and gobbled it down.

"Bad manners!" said Neal. "Here. Try this on for size!" He ran over with a garden bucket and dropped it over the Ninn's head. "Yep. It fits!"

Keeah sent a blast of blue light at four more Ninns, tumbling them over the patio wall.

"Get the boy!" two new warriors grunted, chasing Eric across the yard to the swing set. He jumped onto the swing, pumped twice, and kicked both warriors as they lunged.

"Bombs away!" said Julie, pummeling the downed Ninns with ripe apples.

"More warriors in the front yard!" chittered Max. He scurried up to the roof and shot a sticky net over another troop of Ninns there. They fell to the ground with a resounding thud.

"Eric, get on!" came a yell from the street.

He turned, and suddenly there was Keeah, popping a wheelie on Julie's bicycle. "What —"

"More Ninns behind you! Come on!"

He climbed over the fence, jumped on the seat behind Keeah, and she tore off around a corner.

"Wow, you're a fast learner!" he said.

"When you fight evil, you sort of have to be. Watch out!" She sent a sparkling blue blast at a troop of Ninns charging from behind a garage. "I am definitely going to ask Friddle to help me build one of these! Now, to your house!"

She pedaled swiftly down the street. But another squad of Ninns leaped from behind a hedge and blocked the way. Yelling, they charged the children, the ground thundering beneath their feet.

Suddenly, they stopped charging, but the thundering went on.

Eric looked at Keeah. "What is that noise?"

Then a tiny voice cried out, "Eric! I promised we would help!"

A moment later, a caravan of blue shovel-nosed beasts came stomping around the corner. And, piled on their backs, an army of hoobahs, tootling their musical instruments as loudly as they could. The beautiful melody filled the air.

"Akkk!" cried the red warriors. "Hate music!" They dropped their weapons and stopped their ears with their chubby fingers.

"Yahoo!" yelled Eric as he and Keeah wheeled toward his house. "Thank you."

"No, thank *you!*" cried Pikoo, waving from atop the largest of the blue beasts.

Keeah pedaled up to Eric's yard just as

Julie, Neal, and Max got there. Together they charged up to his door. Suddenly, the sky flashed with red light, and the air grew hushed.

Eric turned. "Something's wrong."

"Galen said to get to Droon," said Keeah.

Eric shook his head. "The Moon Medallion. Sparr will hurt Galen. I have to go back." He started to run.

"Eric!" yelled Keeah. "Eric, wait!"

But he was already rushing back through the yards to Main Street. When he got there, Galen was standing in front of the library. He held up his hand. "Eric, you should not have come back."

"I had to."

"Then get behind me," said Galen.

Sparr strode slowly toward them, the Moon Medallion flashing in his hand.

Galen stared at the stone. "You stole that."

The sorcerer broke into a cold grin. "Such a strange family we have. Urik and I met in the past. We fought. I took the moonstone. Demither told me about the branch that would strike me down. But this has power over the sons of Zara. I can break the branch."

"You talk too much," said Galen. But even as he sent a blast at Sparr, an icy-white mist seemed to swirl from the stone, shoot across the air, and encircle the old wizard. He sank to the street.

"Ha!" crowed Sparr. "It does work! And look. You no longer stand in my way, old man!"

Galen gasped for breath. His face grew as pale as the stone itself. His eyes closed, and crystals of ice began to form on his skin.

The children and Max rushed up the street, looking on with horror. Even as the noon sun shone down, it seemed as if Galen were turning to ice right before them.

Trembling, Eric knelt down next to Galen. He took the wizard's hand in his own. He nearly dropped it again. Galen's hand was warm. In fact, it was hot. Eric looked down to see a thin stream of silver light coil away from the wizard's fingers and swirl through the mist toward the sorcerer.

"Galen?" he whispered.

"Go, Eric. Escape," said the wizard softly, pulling him closer. "You are young . . . strong . . . like the branch of a mighty tree."

"No! No, this can't happen."

"But it is happening!" said Sparr.

Eric turned to stare at him, but what

caught his eye was the medallion itself. Its strange symbols, carved so deeply into the surface, were glowing with silvery light.

Eric couldn't believe his eyes. For a moment, he almost believed that Galen was *drawing* the medallion's icy frost over himself. But why? *Why?*

"Leave me," whispered Galen, staring right at Eric. "Take the Viper. Hide it away. Both our worlds will thank you. Lives are at stake."

At that moment, looking into Galen's eyes, Eric seemed to understand what was happening. Somehow, Galen was doing this for him. So he could escape.

Eric shook his head. "Lives are at stake," he said. "But not yours, Galen. Not today. You have lots of years left. Lots of time to stop Sparr. Together, we'll get him. We will. Because we're the good guys."

Eric stood and unhooked the Viper

from his belt. "You want this, Sparr? Here. Take it!"

He tossed the crown roughly at Sparr.

Sparr laughed. As he grabbed the Viper, the Moon Medallion's white cloud vanished instantly. And in that moment, Galen leaped to his feet and pulled the stone from Sparr's neck.

"Take the trinket!" cried Sparr. "I have the Viper!"

He turned the crown slowly in the air. As he did, it began to hiss menacingly and cast its golden light on the faces of everyone present.

"Eric, I never thanked you for fulfilling the prophecy," Sparr sneered. "How kind of you to find the Viper and bring it to me!"

Eric stared at him. "Here's another prophecy for you, Sparr. Whatever your big plan is, you'll lose. And we'll be the ones to stop you. All of us. Count on it."

His sneer fading, Sparr lifted the crown high. "Ninns! I have my Coiled Viper! Our work here is done. Quickly now, we go to the rainbow stairs. We go — to Droon!"

The Ninns cheered. "Sparr, Sparr, Sparr!"

With a noisy crash of lightning and a giant cloud of smoke, the sorcerer led his chubby warriors down the street and away.

His strength returning, Galen turned to Eric. He held up the Moon Medallion. "Eric —"

"There's no time," said Eric. "Sparr's going to my house. And my parents are home!"

Ten

Sunrise

When they got to Eric's house, it looked like a tornado had struck.

The mailbox had been knocked over, the door was hanging by a hinge, and the kitchen was a mess of macaroni and cheese, crushed soda cans, half-eaten chicken tenders, and melting ice cream.

"Uh, Eric," said Neal as they raced in, "either your parents are getting sloppy or the Ninns just discovered your fridge."

"Give me that mustard!" snapped a voice.

"Those are *my* cookies!" snarled another.

"My parents!" Eric gasped.

Galen pulled open the basement door to see Mr. and Mrs. Hinkle struggling with a pair of hungry Ninns on the stairs.

"Excuse me!" Galen grabbed the Ninns by their ears and dragged them down the basement stairs. The kids jumped down after him.

"I'm not sure I like these new friends of yours, Eric!" said Mrs. Hinkle as they passed.

"They aren't my friends, Mom," Eric replied. "They're here to take over!"

"To take over our kitchen?" asked Mr. Hinkle.

"Nope, the world!" said Julie.

When the kids got into the basement,

they saw Sparr pushing a bunch of mustard-squirting Ninns into the closet. "In, you fools!" he cried.

"Wherever you go, Sparr," said Galen, sparks streaming off his fingertips, "we'll find you."

Sparr grinned. "And when you do, I shall be more powerful than you can possibly imagine."

Eric felt anger building up inside of him. "So go ahead. You got the Viper. Put it on. Let's see how much more evil you can look!"

Sparr narrowed his eyes at the children, then laughed. "This crown? Oh, it's not for me."

Galen gasped under his breath. "What?"

"Then who is it for?" asked Keeah.

Instantly, a new expression crossed Sparr's face, one that Eric had never seen there before. It was so strange, he almost didn't know what to make of it. Then he knew. It was fear. It was as if Sparr looked into the future and saw something — or someone — terrifying. Sparr really *was* scared.

The look vanished in a flash.

But Eric had seen it and knew what it was. Sparr turned to the closet.

"One more thing," said Eric.

"Yes?" said Sparr.

"I'll never help you again!" And with a single push, Eric heaved Sparr into the closet and slammed the door.

Ka-whooom! The room exploded in red light, then everything went quiet.

Galen flung open the closet door again. Sparr and the Ninns were gone. "Well done. Now, Max, Keeah, children, follow me!" His strength completely back, Galen leaped down the stairs toward a Droonian sunrise.

Everyone followed close behind, but Sparr's lead was too great. By the time they reached the bottom of the stairs, Sparr and his Ninns were already lifting into the pink sky on a flock of groggles. The flying lizards flapped their heavy wings and turned toward a distant sea.

"He flies away to fight another day," said Max.

"Look," said Keeah, pointing across the sea. A large serpent's tail broke the surface and slapped the water. "It's her. Witch Demither."

Galen nodded. "Yes, she plays a part in this mystery of the Coiled Viper. Keeah, you, Max, and I must find out more. And we must do it now. There is no telling what wickedness Sparr will conjure next!"

Eric watched the groggles disappear beyond the horizon, then turned. "Om's words were true. I did give the Viper to Sparr."

"Urik's words came true, too," said Keeah. "Greatness came to you when you needed it most. Besides, no one knew that by giving away the Viper, you would be saving Galen's life."

"But Sparr's more powerful than ever now."

Holding the Moon Medallion in his hand, Galen shook his head. "By giving Sparr the Viper, Eric, by saving me, you made *us* stronger. And what makes us stronger makes Sparr weaker. Now, scoot up to your world. Just before we left, I set a charm on the town. No one will remember today. Except you, of course!"

"Too bad the Ninns left Eric's house a total disaster area," said Neal.

"For that," said the wizard, "you will need an even more ancient technique."

"A cleaning spell?" said Julie. "You really need to teach us that one!"

"Better than a spell," said Galen, winking at Keeah and Max. "Old-fashioned hard work!"

With a wave of his hand, Galen conjured a spinning circle of blue light. "Now, all aboard for Jaffa City. We must plan our next adventure!"

"Plan on us being there, too!" said Eric.

Keeah laughed as she stepped into the swirling light. "We wouldn't have it any other way!"

A moment later, the wizard, the spider troll, and the princess were gone.

The three friends raced back up to Eric's house, where they found his parents sitting at the kitchen table, dazed and wondering why there were mustard stains all over the basement.

Eric laughed. "Mom, Dad, we'll clean up the mess. But there's something we need to do first."

He turned. Julie and Neal were smiling.

"To the alley!" they said.

Ten minutes later, the three friends stood between the brick walls at the entrance to Calibaz.

Neal took the flute from his pocket and played Pikoo's tune once more.

The air barely rippled this time, but as long as it did they could see beyond the veil.

"Oh, no," said Julie.

The tents were gone. The streets were gone. Everything was gone. Only scraps of fabric here and there and the trampled ground showed that anything had ever been there.

The sea, as vast and stormy as before, rolled darkly all the way to the horizon.

"Good-bye, Pikoo," Eric whispered.

Neal stopped playing, and the air went still. The alley was an alley once more.

"Do you think we'll ever see Calibaz again?" asked Julie. "Or Pikoo and his hoobah friends?"

Eric imagined the hoobahs living unknown to everyone on the far side of the veil, playing their music, living in their colorful tents, hoping, waiting, dreaming. He wondered if their legend was just a legend or if it would really come true. Would a stranger lead them to this side to stay?

"Maybe someday," he said.

"At least we have this cool souvenir," said Neal, slipping the strange little flute into his pocket. "To remember what happened today."

Julie laughed. "As if we'll ever forget the day Sparr came to town!"

"Or the creepy way the Coiled Viper hissed at us," added Neal.

Eric shivered. "Or the moment when Sparr said the crown wasn't for him."

The three friends stared at one another.

"Come on," said Neal. "Let's clean up your closet. I have a feeling we'll be using it again very soon!"

Without another word, the three friends raced to Eric's house to get to work.

ABOUT THE AUTHOR

Tony Abbott is the author of more than fifty funny novels for young readers, including the popular *Danger Guys* books and *The Weird Zone* series. Since childhood he has been drawn to stories that challenge the imagination, and, like Eric, Julie, and Neal, he often dreamed of finding doors that open to other worlds. Now that he is older — though not quite as old as Galen Longbeard — he believes he may have found some of those doors. They are called books. Tony Abbott was born in Ohio and now lives with his wife and two daughters in Connecticut.

For more information about Tony Abbott and the continuing saga of Droon, visit *www.tonyabbottbooks.com*.

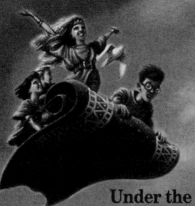